Little Gift

Hello my name is Little Gift
and I am a Giant Panda.

My mama named me Little Gift because I'm super special to her!

I look small now . . .

... but I'm going to grow up to be as big as my mama one day.

I was born in a zoo, because I am an endangered species.

An endangered species is any type of plant or animal that is in danger of disappearing forever.

There are only about 1000 pandas alive in the world today.

Panda in Chinese is spelled like this and means "big bear cat."

A lot of my family lives in Western China and Tibet inside bamboo forests—

—but my mama and I live here at the zoo!

All of this talking about pandas is making me hungry; but what do pandas eat?

Bonita the Fruit Bat offers me some cherries, but that's not what pandas eat!

Squire the Squirrel brings me an acorn,
but that's not my kind of treat.

Bubbles the Buzzing Bumble Bee brings me a flower,
"Does that sound good to eat?"

No! Pandas only eat one thing and mama knows it's true.
Long and leafy, green and crunchy, pandas eat bamboo!

Learning is fun; ready for another story?
Let's Go!

Inside Out
Corn

What's this; it looks like
a little cloud.

Mama! Look what
I found on the ground.

One of the visitors
here at the zoo
must have dropped
some popcorn.

Let me teach you about popcorn Little Gift.

Popcorn is a food people like to eat.
Popcorn doesn't start out looking
like this little cloud.

Popcorn starts out as a kernel from a cob of corn.
Every corn cob is covered with seeds.

The seeds are called kernels. Popcorn kernels are wrapped in a shell which is airtight.

The seed is inside the kernel along with a little water.

The fun part to watch is when a popcorn kernel is heated, the water inside turns to steam.

The steam creates pressure inside the kernel, causing it to burst.

It's an explosion strong enough to turn the seed inside out!

Popcorn is a seed turned inside out!

Wow Mama!
Do you think I
would like popcorn?

Well baby boy, you can try it?

Yuck! I like bamboo a lot better.

But this was really fun to learn about anyway...thanks Mama!

Coloring Time!

GIANT PANDA
Scientific Name: *Ailuropoda melanoleuca*

Bonnie Lee Books

bonnieleebooks.com